To my mom, who read to me.

And to my dad, who let me choose any book I wanted. —R.C.

For the books that I devoured and to the family that fed my obsession,
thank you for wrapping me up in your stories. —M.C.

Library of Congress Cataloging-in-Publication Data

Names: Cole, Rachael, author. | Crowton, Melissa, illustrator.

Title: Mousie, I will read to you / Rachael Cole ; illustrated by Melissa Crowton.

Description: First edition. | New York : Schwartz & Wade Books, [2018]

Summary: "Follows a mama mouse and her baby mouse on the little mouse's journey to becoming a reader—
from infancy to toddlerhood to elementary school and beyond"—Provided by publisher.

Identifiers: LCCN 2017043724 (print) | LCCN 2017057098 (ebook) | ISBN 978-1-5247-1538-0 (ebook)

ISBN 978-1-5247-1536-6 (hardcover) | ISBN 978-1-5247-1537-3 (library binding)

Subjects: | CYAC: Books and reading—Fiction. | Mother and child—Fiction. | Growth—Fiction. | Mice—Fiction.

Classification: LCC PZ7.1.C643 (ebook) | LCC PZ7.1.C643 Mou 2018 (print) | DDC [E]—dc23

The text of this book is set in 19-point Kepler.

The illustrations in this book were rendered digitally.

MANUFACTURED IN CHINA

2 4 6 8 10 9 7 5 3 1

First Edition

Random House Children's Books supports the First Amendment and celebrates the right to read.

MOUSIE, I WILL READ TO YOU

WRITTEN BY

RACHAEL COLE

ILLUSTRATED BY

MELISSA CROWTON

schwartz & wade books · new york

Long before the words make sense, Mousie,

I will read to you

The simplest story

About an acorn that drops to the ground.

While we are rocking,

I will whisper in your ear

A sentence

About a soft rain coming down.

When summer comes,

And you are tired from swinging on the swings,

I will sing you

A lullaby

About the sun fading slowly

While the sky fills with stars.

In the middle of the night,

When your crying fills the room,

I will read you

A poem

About the quietest forest,

Where the only sounds are the crickets,

Whispering *sh-Sha sh-Sha*

Just for you.

When morning comes,

I will fill your listening ears with words

About sun drying dew off the grass

And clearing away the cold and dark of night.

Before you know it, Mousie,

Your DAA DAA DEEs and BAA BAA BEEs

sound like jazz.

I will answer back as you smile,

With words that echo yours,

Like DADDY and BUMBLEBEE.

Your first words fall out of your mouth like treasures—

DADA, BABY, BYE-BYE.

I will scoop them up

And write them down.

Soon after you turn two,

On a foggy neighborhood walk,

You tell me, "There! A tree!"

And I will answer, "It's a strong oak.

The squirrels love to play in it."

After bathtime, cozy in pajamas,

You'll climb into my lap,

Asking for the book about the bear.

The day falls away.

It's just you

And me,

And the rhythm of the words.

I will take you to a library near a playground.

And now that you're a big boy,

You will pick out your own book.

And while sitting on a bench outside,

You will surprise me by reading a word.

Then two,

Then three.

Years later,

I will find you,

With a flashlight in your room,

Reading a chapter book

To your stuffed animals.

I will quietly close the door

And leave you be.

On a spring evening walk,

We will discover that you are taller than me,

Then talk about the stars, the planets,

And where we all come from.

And when you are grown,

You will read about things

I've never known

And haven't dared to dream.

Then one day, before you know it,

On a blanket in a forest,

You will read a story

To *your* baby . . .

. . . about an acorn that drops to the ground.

RAISING A READER

When parents talk, read, and sing with their infant or toddler, connections are formed in young brains, and the bond between parent and child is strengthened at a critical time in the child's development. Studies have shown that these simple acts build language, literacy, and social-emotional skills that last a lifetime. The American Academy of Pediatrics advises parents to read with their children every day, from the time they are born for as long as they both enjoy this special activity, even into the teen years.

Here are a few tips to make reading together fun for all:

- Follow your child's lead. Let him or her choose a book and then encourage the child to hold it, turn its pages, pat it, or even taste it as is developmentally appropriate.

- Don't try to make this time longer than keeps your child's interest; eventually children will want you to keep reading all night, but don't push it.

- Count things; name things; point out details in the art.

- Guess what will happen next in the story and talk about what the characters might be thinking and feeling. Talk about how you might tell a similar but different story—*your* story.

- Make reading together part of your daily routine, perhaps at bedtime. This will become the best twenty minutes of your day!

- Being read to is fun for people of all ages, so even when children start reading on their own, keep offering to share a book with them.

—Pamela High, MD
Fellow, American Academy of Pediatrics

Divali Rose

Vashanti Rahaman

ILLUSTRATED BY

Jamel Akib

BOYDS MILLS PRESS

HONESDALE, PENNSYLVANIA

Text copyright © 2008 by Vashanti Rahaman
Illustrations copyright © 2008 by Jamel Akib
All rights reserved

Boyds Mills Press, Inc.
815 Church Street
Honesdale, Pennsylvania 18431
Printed in China

CIP data is available

First edition
The text of this book is set in 13-point Palatino.
The illustrations are done in oil pastel.

10 9 8 7 6 5 4 3 2 1

In memory of my father's parents, Bajnath and Moon Ramcharan
—*V.R.*

For Pea, Bean, and Mitch
—*J.A.*

RICKI WAS LEAVING FOR SCHOOL when he saw the two rosebuds. They were on the bush he had helped Grandpa plant. Whenever Ricki asked what color the new roses would be, all Grandpa would say was "Divali color for a Divali rose."
Ricki could not imagine what Divali color might be.

So he gently bent the tip of one bud, hoping to see a hint of color—and the rosebud snapped off!

Fear and worry darkened Ricki's mind. At first his feet refused to move. Then he raced down the path to school.

Even his art teacher talked about Divali. "This is a time to remember that we can all be lights, chasing away the darkness of fear and worry," she said as they got ready to paint.

Ricki painted a single *deeya*, or oil lamp, near a single rosebud.

That evening, Grandpa was grumpy.

"Somebody meddled with his rosebush," said Grandma.

"I tell you is the India people," said Grandpa. "Who else it could be?"

"And I tell you not to accuse people of mischief just because they different," said Grandma.

Ricki decided that this wasn't a good time to talk about the rosebud accident.

Grandpa began guarding the rosebush day and night. Ricki sat with him often and watched the remaining rosebud open a little more each day. On the inside, the red petals were streaked with yellow and orange. "You see?" Grandpa said. "Divali color is the color of fire."

Whenever the India people's children passed by the house, Grandpa jumped up shouting, "See them watching? Waiting for me to *stop* watching?"

Then Ricki would think, *Tomorrow will be a better time. I'll tell him about it tomorrow.*

On the night before Divali, Ricki asked Ma, "Why Grandpa is always blaming India people for something and saying how they different and bad? They is Indian, just like us."

"Not just like us," said Ma, putting water on to boil for evening tea. "They only just come here. Our family come from India more than a hundred years ago."

"But even if they is different, that is no reason for Grandpa to be afraid of them," said Ricki.

"You right, child," said Ma.

Ricki took the tea to Grandpa and watched him sip it.

"You know that picture your grandma have of her father and mother?" said Grandpa after a while.

"The one on her dresser?" asked Ricki.

"Bring it here," said Grandpa.

"Now, them is real Indian," said Grandpa. "Them people who only now come from India—they not like that at all."

"But we not like that, either," said Ricki. "I don't think I could be like one of those long-ago people that first come from India to Trinidad."

"Me neither," said Grandpa. "Is not easy to leave home and go someplace where you different from everybody else. Them long-ago Indian people didn't have it easy when they first come here. My own grandfather used to tell me about it. They didn't have it easy at all."

"Just like them new India people, eh, Grandpa?" said Ricki.

"So . . . what they teach you about Divali in school?" asked Grandpa, changing the subject.

"One teacher say Divali come like a new year,"
said Ricki. "You have to make peace with everyone and
start new for the new year."

Grandpa was quiet for a long time. Finally, he sat up.
"You and that teacher have a point," he said. "Come with me."

"But I have something to tell you," said Ricki.

"Later," said Grandpa.

Grandpa took out his pocketknife and cut the stem of the Divali rose.

"What are you doing?" cried Ricki.

"Come," said Grandpa.

Ricki followed him down the road to the India people's house.

A woman opened the door and Grandpa gave her his rose. "It is clean, no pesticide," he said. "You can use it however you want. But when you send the children in my yard for flowers for your prayers, you must tell them to ask me instead of picking the flowers themselves. That is how we do things here."

"That is how we do things, too," said the woman. With a puzzled look, she took the rose. "I would never send them to pick other people's flowers without asking first."

"Then who meddled with my new rosebush?" asked Grandpa.

"It was me," whispered Ricki. "That is the thing I was trying to say."

The India lady smiled at him gently. "Don't be afraid," she said. "You are a good child."

Grandpa and Ricki walked home in silence.

The next evening, after prayers, Ma and Pa filled new deeyas with coconut oil. Grandpa and Ricki followed after them with cotton wicks. Finally, Grandma lit the little lamps. Then they watched as neighbors lit deeyas too, along railings and walkways. Ma had just gone in to set out dinner when a boy came up the front steps. He gave a covered dish to Grandma and quickly ran off.

Grandma lifted the lid. "The India people send their special milk sweet," she said to Grandpa.

Ricki saw that the dish was filled with little white balls, made from milk curds, soaking in syrup. There was something else, too. "Grandpa!" he cried. "Look!"

Floating on the syrup were the flamelike petals of the Divali rose.

"Ah!" said Grandpa to Ricki. "Those India people are good neighbors, not so?"

Ricki smiled, and for the first time since he had broken off the rosebud, fear and worry faded from his mind.